BE A DETECTIVE!
A Mystery a Minute for You to Solve

MYSTERIES for CRIME-BUSTERS

By the Editors of Read Magazine,
a Xerox Education Publication
With Illustrations by Jody Taylor

inkpot books
GROSSET & DUNLAP
A FILMWAYS COMPANY
Publishers • New York

CONTENTS

INTRODUCTION

How good a detective are you? Can you compete with Police Captain Tom Reilly? He's an expert when it comes to recognizing clues and making logical deductions.

It's all elementary for him!

How about you? If you read carefully you should find at least one and often several clues in each of the mini-mysteries that follow. Then, after you've come to your own conclusion, turn to the back of the book for Captain Reilly's solution and an explanation of how he arrived at it.

STAIN ON THE RUG

It had been two days since Lieutenant Lanzi and Captain Reilly had rescued Sergeant Ann Gerritts from a terrorist gang, and Gerritts was glad to be back at work. But the case Captain Reilly assigned to her was a real stumper. It involved the death of murder-mystery writer Herb Michaels.

"It all adds up to suicide, Chief," Gerritts said to Reilly. "Except —"

"Yes, I know," replied Reilly. "Except how? *How* did Herb Michaels hang himself?"

Reilly stared down at the open file on his desk. "The report indicates that no chair, stool, or support of any kind was found below or near the spot where Herb Michaels' body was hanging. So how did he do it?"

"Where was he found, Chief?" Gerritts wanted to know. "I know it was somewhere in his living room, but *exactly* where?"

"His body was hanging from a rope that had been looped over a beam in the ceiling," Reilly replied, getting up to pace around his desk. "The beam was next to the brick fireplace wall."

"Hmm," said Gerritts. "And he'd been dead how long?"

"The coroner says about twelve hours," Reilly replied. "And the ashes in the fireplace were still slightly warm, which makes it seem that he made a fire right before he died."

"Well, it doesn't make sense," sighed Gerritts. "I mean, if it *was* murder, why didn't the murderer make it look like suicide? Why didn't he or she leave a chair or something under the body?"

"And if it was suicide," said Reilly, "what did Michaels stand on?"

Reilly strode back to his desk. "Let's look at the photos again," he said.

"Okay," said Gerritts. She leaned over to get a closer look. "I don't see anything unusual," she said, "except for the darkish stain on the carpet. What is it, Chief?"

"According to the lab reports, it's a big water stain," said Reilly.

"Oh? Well, there *has* been a lot of rain lately," said Gerritts. "Maybe Michaels' roof leaks."

"Maybe," said Reilly, getting a sudden thought. "But I don't think so. No, I think Herb Michaels killed himself in a very clever way. I'm not sure why he did it, except to stump us. He *was* a mystery writer, after all. But I think I know how."

How does Reilly think Michaels may have committed suicide?

RING AT THE DOOR

It was late afternoon when the snow began. It continued all night. By morning, snow was piled knee-high, and hundreds of power lines sagged and snapped under the weight.

Police Captain Tom Reilly had just finished the last day of his ski vacation and had planned to return home. But now the airport was closed. Reilly was in a gloomy mood as he paced back and forth in the airport corridor, waiting for service to resume. Suddenly a short man dashed up to Reilly.

"Excuse me, sir," the man said breathlessly. "You're Police Captain Tom Reilly, aren't you?"

"Why, yes," Reilly answered. "Can I help you?"

"I believe you can," the man said. "I'm Sam Jenkins, the police chief here. And I can use your help in solving a robbery."

"But I'm on vacation," Reilly protested. "Well, actually, I've just finished my vacation, and I'm on my way home."

"By the time the weather clears, you'll have the crime solved," Jenkins said.

Jenkins quickly drove Reilly to the scene of the crime — the home of Robert Peterson, a wealthy businessman, where the power was out because the lines were down. Once there, Reilly checked through the dark house, looking for clues. In the living room, near a broken window, Reilly stepped on some glass.

"I've got a suspect," Jenkins said. "But I might not have enough evidence to charge him.

"Caught him about three blocks from the Peterson house," Jenkins continued. "He had an expensive cigarette lighter in his pocket with the initials R.P. on it. And his billfold bulged with enough money to choke a

8

horse. One of Peterson's neighbors saw this man leaving through Peterson's front door about the time of the robbery. We caught up to him a little later in a restaurant."

"I'm Carl Benton, and I'm innocent," the man pleaded. "Sure, I was at the Peterson house. I'm a salesman, mostly cleaning and kitchen gadgets.

"I came to the house and rang the door bell. I heard it ringing, but no one came to the door. As I started to leave, a man crashed through a window and ran away. He dropped this lighter, and I picked it up. Everything seemed strange, but I didn't want to be blamed, so I left quickly."

"How about all that money?" Jenkins asked.

"I earned every cent of it," Benton answered. "I've sold a lot of gadgets today."

"I'm afraid you're going to be out of business for a while," Reilly said. "I suggest you charge this man with robbery, Mr. Jenkins."

What clues tipped Reilly off?

BITTER ALMONDS

Richard Compton, a distinguished corporate executive, had been dead only a few hours when Police Captain Tom Reilly and Sergeant Ann Gerritts arrived at his home.

"Where was the body found?" asked Gerritts, as they entered the oak-paneled foyer.

"In the game room," said Reilly.

Downstairs in the game room, police photographers were snapping pictures of Compton, who sat slumped in a chair. His right hand still held a small cup. His left hand was smeared with ink.

"Any ideas on the cause of death?" Reilly asked the coroner, who was making out a report.

"Cyanide poisoning, I'm sure," replied the coroner. "Which means it hit him like lightning. You can smell the poison in the cup. It has a slight odor like bitter almonds."

A sound on the steps interrupted him. It was Ada Compton, the dead man's wife. She was still sobbing softly.

"Dick had been down here writing letters," she said. "He'd been very depressed recently over a series of bad business deals. But I didn't think he was depressed enough to consider suicide." Mrs. Compton started crying in earnest, her sobs loud and racking.

"There, there," consoled Gerritts, trying to be sympathetic. "Tell me, when was the last time you saw your husband alive?"

"At dinner," Mrs. Compton answered, "a little after seven. He acted normal — a little quiet, perhaps, but not seriously despondent or anything. When we'd finished eating, he said he wanted to write some letters, and so he came down here.

"At ten I hadn't heard a sound from him, so I came downstairs, thinking he might have fallen asleep. What a terrible shock it was to find him this way!"

"Did you touch anything at all after you found the body?" Gerritts asked.

Reilly was looking on with interest.

"No," Mrs. Compton replied. "Nothing."

"In that case," Reilly said, "I think you'd better come along to headquarters with us, Mrs. Compton. On suspicion of the murder of your husband."

Why did Reilly suspect Compton had been murdered?

INTERRUPTED CONFERENCE

"Police Captain Reilly. Police Captain Reilly. There's a phone call for you in the lobby."

It had to be important. Captain Reilly had left strict instructions back at the station that he was not to be disturbed at the National Policemen's Conference in Atlantic City unless it was an emergency.

Pushing his way through the mobs of blue-coated policemen, Reilly finally made it to the house phone. "Yes, Reilly here," he said, a bit out of breath.

"Sorry to bother you sir," the lieutenant on the other end said. "But we thought you would want to know that your friend Roger O'Malley is dead."

"Roger — dead?" Reilly said in disbelief. "How did it happen?"

"Well, sir, we think he committed suicide. Mr. O'Malley's partner, George Thompson, found him dead in his office last evening. He had been shot in the right temple."

"That doesn't sound like suicide to me, Lieutenant," Reilly said harshly.

"Oh, I'm sorry, sir. I forgot to tell you that O'Malley left a note in the typewriter."

"A note?" Reilly asked. "What did it say?"

"Well, not much, sir. It said that he was tired of life and wanted to end it all."

"I don't believe it. I just don't believe it." Reilly muttered to himself.

"Pardon, sir? I couldn't hear you."

"Nothing. Nothing." Reilly answered. "What about the gun? Was it O'Malley's?"

"Yes, sir. We found it on the floor on the left side of his chair and we immediately checked the registration. It was his all right."

"What about fingerprints?" Reilly asked with growing impatience.

"We ran a fingerprint test on it, sir, and found nothing."

"How did Thompson happen to find O'Malley, Lieutenant?"

"Well, sir, he said that he had forgotten some very important papers that he was going to work on that night, so he went back to the office. When he saw a light in O'Malley's office, he went in and found him dead. That was at about ten."

"Okay, Lieutenant. This is what I want you to do. Call Mrs. O'Malley, and tell her I'll be there in three hours. Meanwhile, I want you to pick up Mr. Thompson for questioning."

"You mean it wasn't suicide?" the lieutenant asked.

"That's right," Reilly said.

Find two reasons why Reilly knew O'Malley hadn't killed himself.

FOOTPRINTS AT THE WINDOW

Police Captain Tom Reilly and Sergeant Ann Gerritts were standing outside the two-story house. On the second floor, curtains moved gently in the breeze from an open window. But everything else was still.

"Don't you see what I mean, Captain?" Gerritts asked impatiently. "The person who stabbed Arthur Warner to death came in and then left by the window. All the clues are here — the footprints over there in the dirt, and the blood on the drainpipe."

Reilly bent down and peered at the footprints in the soft earth. The prints, deeply stamped into the ground, seemed to have been made by a man's shoes. One set pointed toward the house. Another shallower set seemed to turn toward the lawn.

"Tell me again, Gerritts," said Reilly. "All entrances were locked?"

"Yes," said Gerritts. "Every door in the house was locked from the inside, and so was every window. Every window except the one in Arthur Warner's bedroom."

They both looked up again at the open window. Directly outside the window was a small terrace.

"We found bloodstains on the drainpipe, right over there," said Gerritts, pointing. Reilly could see them clearly. They stopped about 8 feet off the ground.

"We also found bloody scratches on the outside edge of the windowsill," Gerritts continued.

"Who was in the house at the time Mr. Warner was murdered?" asked Reilly.

"His wife," answered Gerritts, "and a couple of members of the household staff, too. But we've checked them all out, and nobody really seems to have had a motive.

"Besides," Gerritts added, "Arthur Warner had been an invalid for five years. Anyone in the house would have had plenty of opportunity to kill him at any time, without going through all this trouble."

Reilly started toward the front door. "Well, I think there's a good chance it's an inside job," he said, "and if you'll look carefully at the evidence, I think you'll see what I mean."

What made Reilly suspect that Arthur Warner's murder had been an inside job?

SHOT IN THE DARK

Captain Reilly wiped the sweat from his brow as he turned to face the breeze coming through the window.

"Sure is hot today," he said to the man standing next to him.

"You can say that again," the man replied. He took out a handkerchief and mopped the back of his neck.

Reilly looked down at the body of Harry Klein. It was face down on the floor of the small photo darkroom. Two gunshot wounds marred the back of the once-clean white shirt.

"Would you like to explain what happened?" Reilly asked.

"It all happened so quickly," Bob Rogers began. "Harry and I entered the darkroom at noon to develop a roll of film. In fact, we had already developed one or two of the prints.

"Before I knew what was going on, a man stopped by the window outside, pulled out a revolver, and shot four times at us through that open window right there. Harry fell to the floor."

"Then what did you do?"

"I ducked into a corner," Roger said. "Then I threw a pan of photo chemicals at the window, and the man ran away. You can still see the liquid splattered on the wall and windowsill. There's even some on the ground outside. And here are the four ejected shells."

"I see," Reilly mused, looking at the shells that Rogers handed him. "What do you think the man wanted?"

"The roll of film, of course."

"What for?" Reilly asked.

"Well, Harry and I were on a secret job to cover a mob attack in a restaurant. We were lucky enough to get close-ups of some of the gang members. The police would have no problems tracking them down because of our photos."

"Tell me, Mr. Rogers," Reilly asked, "did you touch anything in this darkroom — anything at all?"

"Absolutely not."

"And another thing," Reilly continued, "why was that film so important?"

"It was our big break," Rogers answered. "We'd been having problems with money lately, and we finally got a real good scoop."

"That's what I thought," Reilly commented. "Sorry I don't believe your story, Mr. Rogers. I think you planned to kill Harry Klein so that you could sell that film back to the mob. Now why don't you just tell me what really happened?"

What two things made Reilly suspicious of Rogers?

MOUNTAIN-ROAD BLOWOUT

Police Captain Tom Reilly had been driving in the mountains all day. It was midnight before he went winding down the steep mountain road in his Volkswagen.

On his way down, Reilly passed several mountain cabins tucked away in the woods. But he never saw anyone. That was why he was surprised when his car's headlights outlined a large automobile parked in the middle of the road.

Reilly hit the brakes, and his small car careened out of control. As he swerved up on the shoulder of the road, Reilly heard his tires blow.

Before he could get out of the VW, three masked men surrounded his car. One of the men jammed a shotgun in Reilly's face and demanded his wallet.

Reilly handed the man his wallet. The three leaped into their car and sped down the road.

After they left, Reilly examined his tires. He picked up a handful of tacks off the road. "That was planned pretty well," he muttered to himself.

Remembering a cabin about two miles back, Reilly started walking. After he had knocked on the door several times, a farmer appeared.

"I was just robbed down the road," Reilly said through the cabin's screened door. "I'd appreciate it if you'd call a garage to get me a new set of tires. And then call the sheriff."

Reilly could hear the man dial the number. "Hello, Okie's Garage? Sorry to get you up at this hour, Okie. Got a man stranded out here. Needs a set of VW tires. Right, see you in a while." The man called the sheriff.

A few hours later, Reilly told his story to the sheriff. Then Reilly turned toward the farmer.

"I'm thankful for this man's hospitality," Reilly said, "But I'm afraid you're going to have to arrest him for robbery."

Why did Reilly suspect that the farmer was one of the masked robbers?

STATUE OF LIBERTY CAPER

Police Captain Tom Reilly received a call to go to New York Harbor. Someone had attempted to break into the vaults at the Statue of Liberty. Two suspects sat awaiting his questioning — a well-dressed man and a scruffy-looking teenager.

Reilly strolled over to where the two people sat under police guard.

"Who are you, and may I ask what you were doing at the statue after visiting hours?" Reilly asked one.

"I assure you, sir," the well-dressed man replied, "I've done nothing wrong. My name is Robert Hobbes. I'm a British historian specializing in American history."

"What were you doing here?"

"I wanted to see this wonderful monument my people gave your country as a gift in 1874. My grandfather was present at the ceremonies when President Harrison dedicated the statue here on Bedloe's Island.

"I meant no harm. I was simply trying to get in. I had no idea the place was closed, you see."

"Yes, I do see," Reilly remarked. Then he turned to the young man in jeans and sneakers. "And what do you have to say?"

"Nothing," the teenager answered. "I was just tossing a Frisbee with some friends here in the park. Then I fell asleep under that tree over there. I figured I had missed the last ferryboat back to New York.

"I don't know why you're asking me these questions," the young man continued. "I haven't done anything wrong. Is it a crime to fall asleep? Either charge me with some crime or let me go."

"I've heard enough," Reilly said. "Come with me."

Which one did Reilly want and for what four reasons?

UNTIMELY END OF BARON VON STREUDEL

It was Christmas Eve, but Police Captain Tom Reilly was still on duty when he received an order to report to the old Von Streudel mansion. Within an hour he arrived at the mansion and entered the main dining hall.

"What's going on here?" he asked.

"Baron Von Streudel's dead," Sergeant Gerritts answered. "We found the body and a gun with the Baron's fingerprints on it. It looks like he shot himself in the right temple."

"Glad to see you're on the job, Gerritts," Reilly said as he examined the crumpled figure of an elderly man dressed in a Santa Claus suit.

"As you know, the Baron was very strange," Gerritts said. "He wore a mask so his servants couldn't recognize him. And he always dressed as Santa at Christmas. Lucky for us the only person who has ever seen the Baron's face is here, or else we wouldn't know for sure who this was."

"I'm André DuBois, the Baron's closest friend," a man said, stepping up to the two. "The Baron often visited my bookshop in the capital of France, where I keep rare books. I've seen the Baron's face, so I was able to identify him. The Baron's death has certainly spoiled my first visit to America."

"You collect rare books in Marseilles?" Reilly asked. "No doubt you have first editions of Poe's play *Moby Dick* and Hemingway's *Jaws*?"

"Of course," DuBois answered.

"I'm Andrew Bennett," another man interrupted. "I was the Baron's banker. I came here for the party and found him face down in the punch bowl."

"The Baron was quite wealthy, wasn't he?" Reilly

asked Bennett.

"At one time he was," Bennett said. "But not now. He wasted his money. He had more debts than he could ever pay. And just before he died, the Baron made a new will. He left a million-dollar insurance policy to his friend, Mr. DuBois."

"Gerritts, take DuBois to headquarters," Reilly said. "And make sure care is taken that his fingerprints are accurate."

"You mean DuBois killed the Baron?" Gerritts asked.

"The Baron may not be dead," Reilly said.

Why did Reilly think the Baron wasn't dead? What clues may have tipped him off?

FREDDIE THE FOX AND THE STOLEN CATS

There had been a robbery at the City Zoo in the middle of the night, and Police Captain Tom Reilly rushed over early the next morning.

"It's just a shame," said Mr. Andrus, the zoo keeper. "Every one of the animals stolen is on the endangered species list. The thief took leopards, cheetahs, and jaguars."

Reilly's jaw was set. "The robber will probably sell the animals' skins for thousands of dollars to unconcerned people," he said grimly. "But I have a good idea of who the thief might be — Freddie the Fox."

Freddie the Fox was a well-known thief whose specialty was hot furs. Reilly had helped put him in prison several times before. But Freddie was out now. Reilly had him summoned to headquarters.

Freddie slouched in his chair.

"Some animals were taken from the zoo last night," Reilly said. "Suppose you tell me where you were."

"Why, I was payin' a visit to my agin' mother, Captain, just like a good son should," Freddie said.

Reilly snorted. "A likely story."

"You wanna call her up and ask her? I got her number right here —"

"No, never mind," Reilly said suddenly. "Maybe I was wrong about you, Freddie. Maybe your friend Rusty the Rat did it."

"Why d'ya say that?" Freddie asked.

"Well, he pulled off a similar job out West a few years ago, didn't he?"

Freddie laughed. "Yeah, that job was myna birds or somethin'. But Rusty's allergic to cats. They make him sneeze."

Reilly smiled. "No, Freddie, Rusty didn't do it. You did. You're under arrest."

How did Reilly know Freddie was the thief?

DEATH BY DROWNING

The short, muscular man stood silently in Police Captain Tom Reilly's office.

"Sit down, Mr. Schultz," Reilly said. "I'm afraid I have some bad news."

"It's my wife, isn't it?" Schultz asked. He sat down heavily on a straight-backed chair. "You've found her."

"Yes." Reilly paused. "That is, we found her body — washed up on the rocks down at Ocean Point."

The man stared into space. "So she finally did it."

"Did what?" Reilly asked.

"Killed herself," Schultz replied. He got up and walked to the window, parting the blinds and gazing out into the street.

"She was always threatening to," he finally said. "She was an unhappy woman. Very unhappy."

"I see," Reilly said. "Mr. Schultz, suppose you tell me about the last time you saw your wife."

"It was two nights ago," Schultz began. "I was on my way out to a meeting, and Sally was soaking in a bubble bath. When I told her I was going out, she became hysterical, screaming that I never paid any attention to her. As usual, she threatened to kill herself."

"And then what happened?" Reilly asked.

"I left the house, upset, of course. I drove around for about an hour before I even got to my meeting. When I came home she was gone."

Reilly leafed through some papers on his desk, pausing when he came to an official-looking folder. "Mr. Schultz, I have here the autopsy report on your wife," he said. "It indicates that death was by drowning, all right," Reilly continued. "But not by drowning in the ocean. I think your wife was already dead when someone threw her into the sea. And I think that someone was you."

What clue in the autopsy report might have given Reilly that answer? How had Mrs. Schultz died?

THE DEADLY SIP

The pine-paneled game room was silent as Police Captain Tom Reilly bent over the body on the floor.

"She's dead," he said, straightening up. "Looks as if she's been poisoned."

He turned to the two men sitting quietly on the long black leather sofa. "Mr. Winters," he said, "suppose you tell me what happened."

The pudgy balding man mopped his forehead with a striped handkerchief. "We were having a drink in front of the fire," he began. "Alice, Harold, and I."

"Who made the drinks? And what was in them?" Reilly interrupted.

"I did," answered Winters. "Alice and I were drinking Scotch and soda, and Harold had a brandy. Anyway, my wife was just sipping at her drink and chatting, and all of a sudden she clutched her stomach and fell over."

Mr. Winters turned away from Reilly. "I see," Reilly said. "Thank you. Can you add to that, Mr. —?"

"I'm Harold Simmons," the other man answered. "It happened just as Ken said. We had been playing cards, and then he made us all a drink. Three-quarters of an hour later, Alice was dead."

"Three-quarters of an hour?" Reilly asked. "Did it take her that long to drink one drink?"

"Alice always sipped her drinks very slowly," Winters put in.

Reilly walked over to the bar and looked at the empty glasses. "I'll have to take these to the lab to have them analyzed," he said. "But meanwhile, Mr. Simmons, I'd like to know if you watched Mr. Winters while he made the drinks."

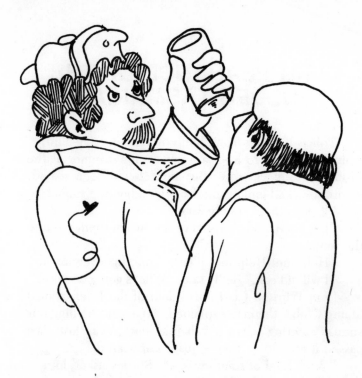

"Yes, I did," Simmons answered. "First he poured in the Scotch, and then he added soda. He mixed them both with a yellow swizzle stick."

"Did he use the same bottles for both drinks?" Reilly asked.

"Yes," answered Simmons. "And then he added some ice cubes."

Reilly looked at Winters. "Do you usually sip your drinks slowly, as your wife did?"

"Why — I — uh——" Winters stuttered.

"Slowly?" Mr. Simmons laughed. "Not old Ken, Captain Reilly. He drank his down in a couple of gulps."

"Then I wouldn't leave town if I were you, Mr. Winters," Reilly warned, heading for the door. "I can't prove it now, but I have a feeling you killed your wife."

How could Winters have done it?

DISAPPEARANCE OF THE GOLDEN TASMANIAN

Police Captain Tom Reilly and Detective Shirley Holmes planned to have a quiet evening dinner at the fabulous Hotel Paradise. But after they'd been seated, loud noises suddenly came from an adjoining room.

"What's that?" Reilly asked.

"Let's see," Shirley said as the two of them ran into the room.

"Help me! Help me, please!" one man screamed.

"I will if I can," Reilly said. "What's going on here?"

"I'm Winston Clark, president of the International Stamp Club," the man explained. "We were holding our annual meeting when a valuable stamp was lost. We passed it around — then it just disappeared."

"What kind of stamp was it?" Shirley asked him.

"An engraved golden Tasmanian," Clark answered. "There are only two of them in the world. I own one, and an elderly collector in Pennsylvania owns the other."

"Have you searched for it?"

"We've looked high and low. We searched under chairs and even vacuumed the carpet. Everyone's been searched — except for this man. He won't allow us to search him."

"And who are you?" Reilly addressed the stranger. "I assume you're a member of the club?"

"My name is Charles A. Charles," the tall gray-haired man replied. "I assure you that I have stolen no one's stamp."

"Mr. Charles isn't a member here," another collector interrupted, walking up to the group. "I invited him to our meeting because he's a great stamp collector. Why his collection is one of the finest in Philadelphia.

"Mr. Charles often carries stamps on his person. I once saw him pull out a rare Mozambique blue stamp to sell to an eager buyer in Boston."

"I know he's got my stamp!" Clark shouted. "I want him searched. I demand police protection!"

"Take it easy, Mr. Clark," Shirley said soothly.

"Oh, Mr. Clark!" someone shouted. "We've found your stamp! It was in an ashtray!"

"I'm really sorry about this, Mr. Charles," Clark said. "But why didn't you want to be searched?"

"I think I know," Reilly said.

If Mr. Charles was innocent, why didn't he want to be searched?

KIDNAPPED!

Outlined in the harsh glare of the police spotlights, the ladder leaned against the back wall of the large Tudor-style mansion. Its legs rested in the soft dirt of the flower bed.

"That's how they got him out," said the gardener. "They took him down the ladder at gunpoint. They had me tied and gagged over there in the bushes."

Captain Reilly nodded gravely and adjusted the brim of his hood to help protect against the spring rain that had been gently falling all day. Next to him stood Mrs. Erickson, sobbing loudly.

"Poor Eugene," she cried.

"When did you notice that your husband was missing?" Sergeant Gerritts asked the weeping woman.

"About nine this evening." Mrs. Erickson answered tearfully.

"Was your husband alone in the house while you were out, Mrs. Erickson?" queried the Captain.

"Yes," she answered. "Jensen, whom you found tied up, had been outside, tending the shubbery. The cook had left right after dinner. And all the doors were locked. My husband is always very careful about securing the house."

"Hence the ladder," Reilly said, looking up to the window. Getting a firm grip on one of the rungs, he took a few steps up the ladder. He glanced down and saw the ends of the ladder sinking into the soft soil of the flower bed. A puzzled expression passed over Gerritts' face.

"Captain, I wish you'd snap out of your daydreams and go out and find my husband's kidnappers," exclaimed Mrs. Erickson impatiently.

"I can give you a full description of the two guys who did it, Captain," Jensen added eagerly.

"I'm sure you could, Jensen. And I'm sure every word of it would be a lie," shot back Reilly. "Just as everything else you've said up till now has been. I think you'd better come downtown, where you can tell us the *real* story."

How did Reilly know the gardener wasn't telling the truth?

NEATNESS COUNTS

Police Captain Tom Reilly walked around the tidy living room. Everything was neat, clean, and in place. The pillows on the corduroy sofa had been plumped up. The pictures on the wall hung straight. And the coffee table had been dusted and polished. In fact, the only disorderly thing in the room was the body on the floor.

The man had been dead about eight hours, Reilly estimated. He looked about forty years old and was fairly tall and thin. His pants still showed a knife-sharp crease in them, and the collar of his light-blue shirt still stood up starchy straight.

On the yellow shag rug next to the man's outstretched right hand lay a pistol. Even without bending down, Reilly could see the neat round hole in the man's right temple.

Lieutenant Lanzi walked over to Reilly. "What've you found?" Reilly asked him.

"Well, the guy's name was Cal Johnson," Lanzi replied. "He was an accountant, not married, and lived alone. From the look of the place, I'd say it was suicide. There's no sign of forced entry anywhere."

Reilly nodded and moved off toward the kitchen area. There he found a tall glass of soda on the counter. Some of it had apparently overflowed, leaving a small, sticky puddle. The rest of the kitchen, like the living room, was spotless.

Back in the living room police photographers were taking pictures of the body. "Did you check around for prints?" Reilly asked Lanzi.

"Yeah. Johnson's are on the glass in the kitchen and all over the rest of the place. No sign of anyone else's."

"How about the gun?" Reilly asked.

"It's clean," replied Lanzi.

"Well, I think we've got a homicide, not a suicide, on our hands," Reilly said. "I think the murderer was someone Johnson knew, and I think Johnson was totally surprised by the attack."

How had Reilly figured all that out?

MURDER ON A SUNDAY AFTERNOON

It was a pleasant Sunday afternoon and Police Captain Tom Reilly was relaxing with a cup of tea and the morning paper when the phone rang. "Isn't there one Sunday or holiday when I don't end up being disturbed?" grumbled Reilly, as he answered it.

"Sorry to bother you, Captain —"

"Yes, yes, I know you're sorry to bother me, Gerritts. Just get to the point."

"My goodness, you're in a dandy mood," Sergeant Gerritts observed. "Well, there's been what looks like a homicide over on Aspen Drive. Bill Korchuk's been shot."

"Korchuk? The mobster?"

"One and the same," Gerritts replied. "And we've got a suspect all ready for you."

"Good work," Reilly replied, his mood improving. "I'll be there in a minute."

George Kennedy, the suspect, was loudly protesting his innocence when Reilly arrived at headquarters.

"Sure I was with Korchuk this morning," he was saying. "I'm the one who found him, remember? But I didn't kill him. I just discovered the body when I got back to Korchuk's house after picking up the paper."

Reilly turned to Gerritts. "What makes you think Kennedy did it?"

"Korchuk was killed at around ten thirty." Gerritts said. "Kennedy says he was at the drugstore, picking up his newspaper then. But we have two witnesses who claim they saw him picking up his newspaper at about nine. And that leaves him no alibi. He's also known to have been an enemy of Korchuk's, and his prints were on the gun," Gerritts finished.

"Are the witnesses here?" Reilly asked.

"I'm here, Captain," a tall, blond woman spoke up. "I saw Mr. Kennedy picking up his newspaper at nine. I'm positive of the time because I noticed the clock on the wall as I walked to the back of the store to complain to the manager."

"Why were you complaining?" Reilly asked.

"I was taking back some ice cream I'd just bought. I could feel how soft it was even through the bag."

Reilly looked at Kennedy. "You may go, for the time being," he said. "Your story may be true."

What made Reilly think Kennedy may have been telling the truth?

MONACO RIPOFF

Awakened in the middle of a blizzardy night, Captain Tom Reilly found himself standing in three inches of snow in front of the just-robbed Hotel Monaco. He was questioning an overly eager witness — cabdriver Frank "Dizzy" Hamchek.

"You were saying something about a runaway car, Dizzy?" the Captain asked.

"Righto, Captain," Dizzy answered. "I mean, I was sittin' here in my cab, readin' tonight's paper. Nothin' much else to do on the graveyard shift, you know, not too many people wantin' cab rides in the wee hours of the mornin'."

"Yes, yes," interjected the Captain. "What happened next?"

"Well, like I say," Dizzy continued, "I was sittin' there reading the paper, and I hear these shots, see, comin' from the hotel. I figure there's somethin' wrong happenin'.

"So then I hear these fast footsteps clompin' like somebody's in a hurry. And when I turn around to get a good look at what's goin' on, I hear this car screechin' and squealin' and makin' all kinds of noise down the street. He musta been doin' eighty! Then he turns that there corner and gets away.

"So like naturally, what could I do? Me, a poor old cabbie. So I call inta headquarters, and they call you, and here you are, and here I am, and that's it, Captain."

"Couldn't you have chased him?" asked Captain Reilly.

"No," Dizzy offered. "I didn't have my motor runnin'. Can't waste no gas, you know. I ain't had no fares for about an hour or so. So, like I said, I called into headquarters, and —"

"Okay, all right," the Captain said. "Mind if we sit in the cab, Dizzy? It's pretty cold out here."

"Sure, Captain," he answered. "It's nice and warm inside the old cab. Best heater in the company."

"Glad to hear that, Dizzy," Captain Reilly said. "Because I'm taking you in on suspicion of robbing the hotel."

What three errors in Dizzy's account made Tom Reilly suspicious?

MURDER ON THE PIER

It was almost midnight, and a cold November wind whipped Police Captain Tom Reilly's overcoat as he walked along the pier. He could hear the low moans of fog horns. But the mist hid any sign of the ships tied up at the dock.

Reilly had been spending a quiet evening, reading a Sherlock Holmes story, when Sergeant Gerritts called him. Someone had been killed down at the dock, and Gerritts needed Reilly's help.

"Chilly out tonight, eh?" Reilly remarked as he approached Gerritts. "Now what's this about a murder?"

"We pulled a sailor's body out of the water a little while ago," Gerritts explained. "His name was Joe Moon. According to some other sailors, Moon was carrying a bag of diamonds."

"I saw Joe get shot," a man standing nearby said. "My name's Carl Benson, and I work on Joe's ship. I was here on the pier when I heard a shot. I looked up just in time to see the flash from a gun. I saw Joe's body fall into the water."

"Did you see who killed him?" Reilly asked.

"Sure," Benson answered. "Robert Jenkins pulled the trigger."

"That's not true," Jenkins interrupted. "I argued with Joe over the diamonds. But I never killed him."

"Argued?" Gerritts said. "Why did you argue?"

"Joe and I worked for six years in Africa," Jenkins said. "We worked in the diamond mines. But we didn't turn all the diamonds over to our employer. We kept a few. After six years, we had enough to equal more than a million dollars. Then Joe wouldn't split the diamonds with me."

40

"I saw Jenkins shoot Joe," another man said. "My name's Sam Peterson, and I'm a sailor, too. I got on board the ship in Australia just a few weeks ago."

"I've always wanted to visit Australia," Reilly said. "But it must be cold there this time of year, too."

"Sure is," Sam remarked.

"The diamonds are missing," Gerritts said. "I'm going to arrest Jenkins for the murder of Joe Moon."

"Don't be so hasty," Reilly said. "You might be on the wrong track."

Whom does Reilly suspect and why?

BLIND MAN'S BLUFF

Shortly after six in the evening, Captain Reilly picked up the phone on his desk and dialed the number of his friend Detective Shirley Holmes.

"Hello?" she answered.

"Shirley," Reilly began, "I have to go out of town for a few days. Can you take a case?"

"What's your hurry, Tom?"

"I have to catch the ferry across the river — the captain said he will leave at oh-seven-hundred hours, and I don't have much time."

"Spill it," Shirley said coolly.

"Three people were trapped in an elevator — one was blind, one was deaf, and one was mute. Then the elevator stopped. The lights went out and somebody screamed.

"When they finally opened the doors, the deaf man was found unconscious on the floor. One of the two men had mugged him — but which? I've already questioned

the blind man, who told me this story. I don't have time to question the other — can you?"

"No need to, Tom," Shirley said. "I know who your chief suspect is — just from your description."

"You do? Who is it?" Captain Reilly was amazed by his friend's quick deduction.

"Why should I tell you?" Shirley snapped. "You're too lazy to take the case."

"But my trip . . . ," he protested quickly.

"Sorry, Tom," Shirley countered. "You're not going on any trip — you just want the evening off. Sometimes you're not careful of what you say."

"But —"

"So long, Tom. I hope you figure out who the culprit is. Meantime, you'd better study your maritime books or you'll be left out on the dock — cold and wet."

Click.

Captain Reilly returned the phone to its receiver.

"How did she know I wasn't going on a trip?" Reilly asked himself. "And who is my suspect? Hmph! Female detectives — bah!"

THEFT OF THE STERLING TROPHY

At four o'clock in the afternoon, Captain Tom Reilly surveyed the broken doors of the intramural trophy case at Store High. Large chunks of glass lay at his feet. Mr. Carter, head custodian, stood by with broom in hand, ready to clean up the mess.

The Captain spoke to two neatly dressed students, captains of rival teams vying for the sterling silver trophy now missing from the case.

"It looks like the doors were hit with a large, blunt object," the Captain said. "Otherwise the glass would have been shattered into tiny pieces."

"Well, I didn't do it," said Pug Barnett, captain of the A Team.

"No one accused you," interrupted Captain Reilly, looking at Pug with suspicion. "But tell me where you were when this happened."

"I was in the gym," Pug said. "I was practicing free throws when I heard this loud crash of glass. Before I could think, I ran out here."

Pug dribbled a basketball as proof of his statement. The ball hit a buckle on his shoe and rolled away.

"How long were you in the gym?" he asked.

"About half an hour," Pug answered.

"He's lying," said Joey Forst, captain of the B Team.

"How do you know?" Captain Reilly asked him quickly.

"Because I was at the pool, looking for my wallet," Joey said. "I know Pug wasn't in the gym because I had been there right before going to the pool. I got here just after the crash, and Pug was already here."

"And did you find your wallet?" asked the Captain.

"I sure did. It was in my gym locker behind the pool." Joey produced the wallet.

"Well," said the Captain, eyeing the two athletes. "One of you is lying — maybe both of you are. But I know the culprit, and he has some questions to answer."

Who broke the glass doors?

HATCHECK SWITCH

Captain Tom Reilly switched off the late news with his remote-control button. He was tired. It had been a rough day down at the station. A glass of warm milk and he would be ready for a good night's sleep.

Just as Reilly was pouring the milk into a pan, he heard a loud pounding on his front door. "That's the trouble with being a detective," Reilly mumbled to himself. "They won't let you alone for a minute."

Tying the sash of his robe snugly, Reilly walked over to the door. When he opened it, he was surprised to see his good friend Brian Sampson.

"Thank heavens you're here," Sampson said, bursting into Reilly's apartment like a hurricane. "You've got to help me."

"What's the problem?" Reilly asked.

"Well, I was out to dinner tonight with George Bennett, Frank Johnson, and Joe Wilcox. When we were leaving Noble's Restaurant, the hatcheck girl handed all of our hats and coats to us at once. Well, somehow they all got mixed up because we're all about the same size and we were all wearing our black evening coats and hats. It turned out that I have Bennett's hat and somebody else's coat."

"Look, Brian," Reilly said, "why don't you just go home and get a good night's sleep? I'm sure that whoever has your hat and coat will call you in the morning."

"No, I need my coat now. I have some important papers in it that I must have tonight."

Not knowing what else to do, Reilly had Brian sit down and call each of the men. After an hour of telephoning, Brian still didn't know who had his coat.

However, this is what he did find out:

1. Each man had the hat of one man and the coat of another. But none of them had his own coat or hat.

2. The man who took Wilcox's hat also took Johnson's coat.

3. The hat taken by Johnson belonged to the owner of the coat taken by Wilcox.

With this information and what Reilly already knew, how did he figure out who had Sampson's coat? Can you also figure out whose hat and coat each of the men had?

SHADOW OF DOUBT

Captain Tom Reilly woke up in a bad mood. Maybe he was getting too old to hack this tough police work.

A robbery had been reported just the day before. It was the third one in a week, and Reilly still didn't have any leads.

The three houses that had been robbed were all in the same neighborhood. In two cases, a big blue truck had been seen in the area. It looked like a one-man operation except for the fact that witnesses had given two different descriptions of the man in the truck.

A neighbor of the first house robbed had seen a bearded man about 5 feet 6 inches. He had been wearing work overalls and had been carrying a TV set out of the house. At the time she hadn't thought anything about it because she knew her neighbors were redecorating. She thought they had just bought a new TV.

In the second case, another neighbor had reported seeing a man over 6 feet tall standing at the back of a blue truck. Actually, she had only seen his shadow.

There was only one thing to do. Reilly jumped out of bed and called Sergeant Gerritts at the station. He told her to bring in Bill Manning and Rod Seagram. Reilly knew that both men had just recently been paroled after serving time for robbery. Bill could fit the shorter man's description, and Rod was a very tall man.

Later at the station, Reilly questioned the two men about their whereabouts on the previous day. Bill said, "Look, Reilly, you got me once, but I'm clean now. You're not going to pin any more robberies on me. I was down at the Town Pool Hall all afternoon and evening. There was this here big match going on. The guys will tell ya I was there."

"I don't know what this is all about," Rod said, "but I couldn't have done anything. My wife and I were with her sick father for the past two days."

Thinking for a minute, Reilly pointed to one of the men and said, "Okay, you come with me."

To whom was Reilly pointing? Why did he think only one man was guilty when there had been two descriptions?

IN THE NICK OF TIME

Captain Tom Reilly wasn't much of a socialite, but on rare occasions he enjoyed a small party with close friends. This evening, his good friend Dave Rumford was having a dinner party at his apartment, and Reilly had been invited.

Since Reilly would be late if he went home from the station first, he decided to go directly to Dave's after work. He knew it would make him early, but that would be all right. It would give him and Dave a chance to catch up on old times before the rest of the guests arrived.

Just as Reilly got to Dave's door, he heard a loud crash, glass shattering, and a hard thump. Something was happening inside — something that didn't sound quite right.

Reilly pounded on the door and started yelling for his friend, but there was no answer. Reilly had only one alternative — he had to break down the door.

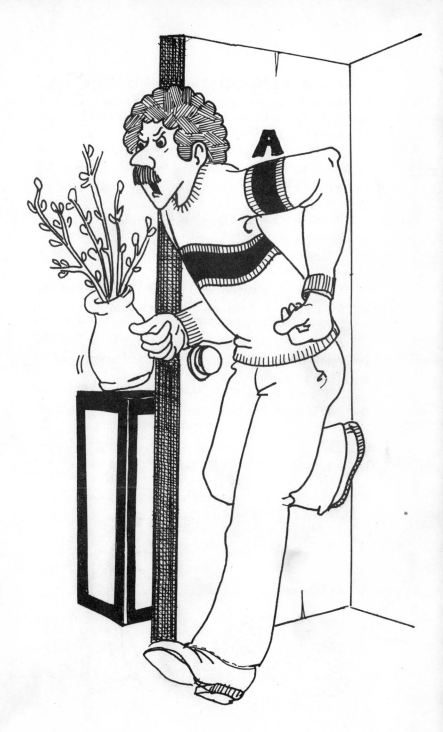

He took a couple of steps back from the door and then lunged forward with all of his 170 pounds. The lock snapped and the force of Reilly's thrust carried him into the living room.

Dave's cat, Hawk, brushed up against him in welcome, but Reilly didn't have time for a friendly greeting. There on the floor lay Mabel and George. A great pool of water surrounded them.

Rushing over to them, Reilly realized that they were still breathing.

"Thank heavens they're still alive," Reilly said to himself.

Quickly glancing around, Reilly noticed that the windows were all closed and the back door had a chain lock. No one could have left.

Just then Dave walked into the living room from the bedroom. "How did you . . .?" he started to say when he saw Mabel and George on the floor.

"What happened? I was just taking a shower. I thought I heard something, but I figured it was only my imagination."

"Well, let's not just stand here," Reilly said. "We need to help Mabel and George before it's too late."

"How did it happen?" Dave asked with concern.

"I think you can answer that yourself, Dave," Reilly said. What had happened and how?

LONG-DISTANCE
DEDUCTION

Police Captain Tom Reilly had been at home with the flu and a cold for three days now. The TV set mumbled in a corner of the room as Reilly sat in bed and thumbed through a magazine. Suddenly the phone rang.

"Hello?" Reilly answered weakly.

"Sorry to bother you, Tom," said Shirley Holmes, "but something has come up at the station, and we need another brain on the job."

"Well," Tom answered with a stopped-up nose, "I'm really not up to it, but I'll see what I can do."

"Just take it easy and listen," Shirley said. "Two men were seen entering Monique's Beauty Salon at about two in the afternoon yesterday. Four minutes later they left — and apparently took the contents of the cash register with them.

"Monique was on the telephone in the back room at the time. The only witness was Mrs. Carter, who was there for her appointment.

"Now you know as well as I that Mrs. Carter's eyesight is very poor. In fact, she wasn't wearing her glasses at that time.

"But we asked her down to the station, and she picked two men out of a line-up. She insists, however, that there were four men. Our two suspects aren't talking — naturally.

"Mrs. Carter's descriptions of the four men seem accurate, but at the same time, they seem puzzling. For instance, she said two of the men were right handed and two were left handed. Only two spoke — the two we

have in custody. And all were about the same height and wore similar dark clothing."

"Where was she when the men were robbing the cash register?" Tom asked.

"She was at the sink in the shampoo area at the back of the room. They tied her hands and faced her to the wall. But she watched the action through a hand mirror propped up on the sink counter.

"According to Mrs. Carter, the place was a mess. The men knocked over bottles that splattered over everything — the floor, two mirrored walls, and chairs."

"Forget the other two men, Shir," Tom said. "The two you have at the station are the only ones."

How did Reilly know?

LOST PRIZE-WINNER

One morning Police Captain Tom Reilly was scanning the newspaper's social pages when the phone rang.

"Captain Reilly?" a shaky voice asked. "This is Emily Taplinger."

"Mrs. Taplinger!" Tom exclaimed. "I just read about your Irish setter, Shawn, winning first prize at the Dog Show. Congratulations!"

"Thank you," she replied somberly, "but my call is not social. You see, Shawn is now missing."

"I'll be right over." *Click.*

Tom raced over to the elegant section of the city, where the Taplinger estate had always been the most beautiful residence in the area.

He drove through rusty gates toward the thirty-room mansion. Tom noticed the tall grass waving in beautiful patterns in the fall wind. He stopped the car, approached the door, and brushed aside some dry vines to ring the bell. Mrs. Taplinger herself opened the door.

"My dear Captain," she said, smiling faintly. "won't you come in? Please wait in the drawing room while I fix some tea."

Tom admired her simple, elegant beauty — noting that she sparkled even without wearing jewelry. He moved into the drawing room and felt its stuffiness. Tom brushed away some dust on the windowsill before opening the window for fresh air. By this time, Mrs. Taplinger had returned with a tea tray.

"One lump or two, Captain?"

"One — but your dog —?"

"Someone has stolen my precious Shawn," she said quietly. "And a woman of my social position cannot bear such a shock, especially today, the servant's day off."

She picked up a napkin and delicately dabbed her nose.

"When did you last see him?"

"After dinner last evening as I cleared the table and straightened the kitchen."

"Was the dog insured?" Tom asked.

"Of course," she snapped, "but money could never replace him."

"I disagree," Tom said abruptly. "I think you've hidden the dog somewhere to get the insurance money."

What eight clues made Tom guess?

ANSWERS

Stain on the Rug

Herb Michaels hanged himself by standing on a block of ice, which quickly melted due to its proximity to the fire. The large water stain on the rug under the body tipped off Reilly to what had happened.

Ring at the Door

Reilly spots two flaws in Benton's statements. First, Benton says that someone crashed through the window from inside the house. But Reilly stepped on glass inside the room, which shows that someone broke into the house. Second, Benton says he rang the doorbell and heard it ring. Reilly notices that the house is dark, since power lines are down; so the doorbell couldn't possibly work. These two clues are enough to tip Reilly off that Benton isn't telling the truth.

Bitter Almonds

Reilly suspected that Compton had not voluntarily drunk the poison for several reasons. First of all, he was holding the cup with his right hand, although the ink smeared on his left hand would indicate he was left handed. And cyanide kills so quickly that it's doubtful that Compton would still be holding the cup. It probably would have dropped out of his hand as soon as the poison took effect. Cyanide's first effect is total muscle relaxation.

Interrupted Conference

The two clues in this episode that lead Reilly to think that O'Malley hadn't committed suicide are: (1) O'Malley was shot in the right temple, yet the gun was found on the left side of his chair; and (2) there were no fingerprints at all on the gun. O'Malley's fingerprints should have been there. Obviously someone else used the gun and then rubbed off the fingerprints.

Footprints at the Window

Nothing suggested that an *entrance* had been made by the drainpipe. All signs indicated the murderer had left that way. Reilly suspected it was an inside job for three reasons: (1) Bloodstains on the drainpipe indicated it had been touched *after* the murder. In addition, the bloodstains stopped about 8 feet above the ground, indicating the murderer probably let go of the pipe and jumped down. (2) Bloody scratches on the outside window also indicated an exit. (3) The footprints' position indicated the murderer probably jumped down, turned, and ran away. Footprints made by an ascending person would not be deep.

Shot in the Dark

Reilly first grew suspicious when Rogers said he had not touched anything in the darkroom. If this were true, the window would have been open when the two men supposedly began developing the film. As a result, the film would have been exposed to light and would be useless. Second, revolvers do not eject shells.

Mountain-Road Blowout

Reilly overheard the farmer calling the garage. The farmer told the garage owner that Reilly needed a set of VW tires. Yet Reilly had not told anyone what size tires he needed. So the farmer must have been one of the robbers.

Statue of Liberty Caper

Reilly arrested Robert Hobbes because Hobbes's story had four main errors that a specialist in American history shouldn't have made: (1) The Statue of Liberty was given to the United States by France not England; (2) The year of the gift was 1884, not 1874; (3) The Statue of Liberty is on Liberty Island. The name was changed from Bedloe's Island several years ago. (4) Harrison wasn't President at the dedication ceremonies — Grover Cleveland was.

Untimely End of Baron Von Streudel

DuBois didn't react to the incorrect authors Reilly gave, and he didn't know the capital of France. As a book collector supposedly living in Paris, DuBois should have known these things. Obviously DuBois is a fake. Then who is he? Reilly suspects he is the Baron in disguise, posing as DuBois so he can collect on his own insurance policy. The Baron would be able to pull such a switch because no one but DuBois knows what the Baron looks like and, similarly, no one but the Baron (at the party) knows what DuBois look like. If DuBois' fingerprints match the prints on the gun, Reilly will be sure that DuBois is the Baron.

Freddie the Fox and the Stolen Cats

Reilly never told Freddie what kind of animals were stolen. Therefore, Freddie's mention of cats gave him away.

Death by Drowning

The autopsy showed that there was fresh water in the woman's lungs. This indicated that she had already been drowned in fresh water — most likely in the bathtub — before the body was placed in the ocean.

The Deadly Sip

Since Simmons had told Reilly that he had seen Winters put ingredients from the same bottles into both drinks, Reilly reasoned that the poison had to have been in the ice. Taking this further, he figured that Mrs. Winters, by sipping her drink slowly, had given the ice a chance to melt, thus releasing the poison. But her husband had avoided drinking the poison by gulping his Scotch down before the ice could melt. Mr.

Simmons wasn't in danger of being poisoned because brandy is practically never served over ice.

Disappearance of the Golden Tasmanian

Mr. Charles didn't want to be searched for the stamp because he was the "elderly collector in Pennsylvania" who owned the other stamp. Reilly realized this when he noted Mr. Charles's gray hair and the fact that he came from Philadelphia. In addition, Mr. Charles apparently always carried valuable stamps on his person, ready to make a quick sale or trade. Had he been searched, Clark would have taken Charles's stamp for the one that the club president lost. And Charles would have had no way of proving Clark was wrong.

Kidnapped!

Reilly knew that Jensen, the gardener, was lying because he claimed to have seen two men take Mr. Erikson out through the window and down the ladder. If this had been true, the ladder would have sunk several inches into the soft wet earth of the flower bed. Reilly found this out for himself when he went up the ladder and noticed it sank under his weight. Since the ladder was not already embedded in the earth, Jensen's story was a lie. Jensen was probably in on the kidnapping.

Neatness Counts

From the look of the house, Reilly could see that Cal Johnson was very neat. Therefore, Johnson would probably not have left a messy puddle of soda pop on the kitchen counter before committing suicide. Also, if Johnson had really killed himself, his own prints would have been on the gun. Obviously, he would have had no opportunity to wipe them off later.

Murder on a Sunday Afternoon

The witness mentioned that the ice cream she'd bought at the pharmacy on the morning of the Korchuk murder had been soft — so soft that she complained to the manager. Reilly reasoned that there might have been a highly localized power failure, affecting only the area around the pharmacy. The power failure could have thrown the pharmacy clock off enough to account for the discrepancy in Kennedy's story.

Monaco Ripoff

Dizzy's account had three errors: (1) Footsteps in three inches of snow are not easily heard, nor (2) could a car screech, squeal, and race down a street in the snow and avoid an accident. In addition, (3) if the cab motor had been off, the heater would not have warmed the cab's interior.

Murder on the Pier

Reilly suspects that Benson and Peterson conspired to kill Joe Moon. Reilly spots three flaws in the two men's stories: (1) Benson says he was on the pier when he saw the murder take place. But the fog was too dense to see the ships tied to the dock. Benson couldn't have seen the murder; (2) Benson says he heard the shot and then saw the flash from the gun. This defies the laws of physics. Since light waves are faster than sound waves, Benson would've seen the shot first and then heard it; (3) Peterson didn't board the ship in Australia or he would've known that Australian weather is the opposite of ours. If it is cold in Reilly's city, it would've been warm in Australia, not cold as Peterson says.

Blind Man's Bluff

Captain Reilly didn't know what he was talking about when he said oh-seven-hundred hours. Sea time is counted on a twenty-four-hour clock, and oh-seven-hundred is seven in the morning. Since he made the call after six in the evening,

Shirley caught him. Tom Reilly *should* have said nineteen hundred hours instead.

Since the supposedly *blind* man told the captain the story, how could he have known when and if the lights went out? He's the chief suspect Shirley Holmes picked out.

Theft of the Sterling Trophy

Pug was lying. He stated he was in the gym, practicing free throws. Yet when he later spoke to Captain Reilly, the basketball "hit a buckle on his shoe . . . ." He was obviously wearing street shoes, something a basketball player would never wear on a gym floor. He broke the glass doors, probably with the basketball itself.

Hatcheck Switch

The easiest way to find the solution to this puzzle is by the process of elimination. Write the men's names vertically on a sheet of paper and start listing the information that is given. Don't overlook Sampson's remark that he has Bennett's hat.

Using the listing method mentioned above, the first thing to put down after Sampson's having Bennett's hat is that Bennett has Wilcox's hat and Johnson's coat. Next would be that Johnson has Sampson's hat, and Wilcox has Sampson's coat. Working it out even further, Sampson has Bennett's hat and Wilcox's coat; Wilcox has Johnson's hat and Sampson's coat; and Johnson has Sampson's hat and Bennett's coat.

Shadow of Doubt

Captain Reilly is suspicious of Bill Manning because Bill says, "You're not going to pin any more robberies on me." From Rod Seagram's remark, it is apparent that the two men had not been told why they were being questioned. Reilly had also figured out that the shorter of the two men might have committed both robberies because one witness had seen only the shadow of the thief. Since it was late afternoon, she might have thought the thief was taller than he really was because the sun casts long shadows then.

In the Nick of Time

The great pool of water, the shattered glass, and the locked apartment should clue the the reader that Mabel and George might not necessarily be human beings. They are, in fact, goldfish. Reilly surmised that Dave's cat Hawk made an attempt at having Mabel and George for dinner.

Long-Distance Deduction

Reilly had been told that Mrs. Carter faced a wall but watched the action through a mirror. Since most beauty salons have mirrored walls (like the one mentioned in this story), Reilly reasoned that Mrs. Carter probably saw reflections of reflections. The mirrors caused her to (a) see four men instead of two, (b) hear two speak and not four, (c) distinguish two right-handed men and two left-handed men (mirror reflections show the opposite), and (d) note that they were all about the same height and wore similar clothing.

Lost Prize-Winner

Mrs. Taplinger, no longer a wealthy woman, needed the dog insurance money to keep up appearances. The clues are: (1) rusty gates, (2) tall grass, and (3) dry vines, all suggesting no gardener; (4) no jewelry, something unbefitting a woman of her "social position"; (5) stuffy room and (6) dust on the windowsill, suggesting that she had not been entertaining guests as would a "social" leader; (7) no servants were employed, as indicated by Mrs. Taplinger's answering the door, fixing the tea, clearing the table, and straightening the kitchen herself; and finally, (8) her calm manner over the missing dog.